BORIS SAVES
THE SHOW

This one is for you T.W. – C.W.

To beautiful Adelaide and Cece – Hip Hip Hooray! – T.W.

OXFORD
UNIVERSITY PRESS

Great Clarendon Street, Oxford OX2 6DP

Oxford University Press is a department of the University of Oxford.
It furthers the University's objective of excellence in research, scholarship,
and education by publishing worldwide in

Oxford New York

Auckland Cape Town Dar es Salaam Hong Kong Karachi
Kuala Lumpur Madrid Melbourne Mexico City Nairobi
New Delhi Shanghai Taipei Toronto

With offices in
Argentina Austria Brazil Chile Czech Republic France Greece
Guatemala Hungary Italy Japan Poland Portugal Singapore
South Korea Switzerland Thailand Turkey Ukraine Vietnam

British Library Cataloguing in Publication Data available

ISBN: 978-0-19-275827-9 (paperback)

10 9 8 7 6 5 4 3 2 1

Printed in China

Paper used in the production of this book is a natural, recyclable product made
from wood grown in sustainable forests. The manufacturing process conforms
to the environmental regulations of the country of origin

For more information about Tim Warnes visit
www.chapmanandwarnes.com

Carrie Weston • Tim Warnes

BORIS SAVES THE SHOW

OXFORD
UNIVERSITY PRESS

The day that Miss Cluck said there was going to be an end-of-term show, everyone was very excited.

At playtime they could talk of nothing else!

Fergus the fox cub
wanted to sing.

Leticia the rabbit
wanted to dance.

Maxwell the mole
wanted to dress up.

And the little mice wanted to do everything!

By lunchtime Boris
was feeling worried.
He had never been in
a show before and
he was rather shy.

He wrinkled his
hairy, scary, grizzly bear
nose nervously and asked,
'Who is coming to watch us?'

'Yes! Yes!'

'Who? Who?'

Everyone looked puzzled.
Everyone looked at Miss Cluck.

'A **very** special audience indeed!' she said. 'I'm inviting Miss Webb and her class from Pond Side Nursery.'

'Yippee!'
'Hooray!'

She gave the important letter to Maxwell and he posted it. With a little help from Boris.

The next day there was great excitement
at Pond Side Nursery when Miss Webb
opened the envelope. She read the
invitation out loud.

'Please come to our school on Friday
for our end-of-term show.
Love from Miss Cluck and Class One.'

Back in Class One it was time to start practising.
Miss Cluck played some notes on the piano.

'Do, re, mi, fa, so!' she sang.
'Your turn,' she said.

'Do!'

'Re!'

'Me!'

'Fa!'

'Soooooooo!'

When Boris sang, all the animals
covered their ears. The piano shook.

'This just won't do!'
sighed Miss Cluck.
'You're much too loud,
Boris dear.'

'Never mind,' spluttered Miss Cluck, 'I've got just the job for a big, hairy, scary, **grizzly bear . . .**'

And she put Boris in charge of making the scenery.

'Don't forget your apron, dear.'

Before long the mice wanted to help, too.

So while Boris painted a great big sun in the sky . . .

they painted tiny little flowers in the grass.

'What a team!'
said Miss Cluck as
she washed the paint
from six little paws
and two great **big** ones.

'Ooops!'

'And now,' said Miss Cluck, 'we must choose our costumes.'

The dressing-up box was full of interesting things to try on.

Tiny hats for the mice,
pretty feathers for Leticia,
a silly wig for Maxwell,
a suit of armour for Fergus,
and just enough
shiny material . . .

Helpful Talk

Ideas

Questions

Team Talk

rns

explaining

to make a
superhero
cape
for Boris!

'Wow!'

The day of the
show arrived.

They were just about to have one
last practice when the telephone rang.

'Hello!' said Miss Cluck.
'Oh dear! What a shame!'

She looked very serious as she put down the phone.

'Bad news I'm afraid,' she said. 'Miss Webb and her class have got stuck in some mud and they won't be able to come to our show after all.' The animals gasped.

'Oh no!'

'They're stuck in the mud!'

'Who will rescue them?'

Suddenly, Boris had an idea.

With a swish of his cape, he hurried outside.

Boris knew a shortcut
through the woods.

He ran and ran and ran with his
cape flying in the wind until . . .

he found Miss Webb
and her nursery class.

The tractor wheels
were stuck fast.
The frogs and
ducklings looked
very glum.

Boris pushed.

He heaved.

He got splattered from head to toe.

But he got them out of the mud!

'What a hero, Boris!'
said Miss Webb.
'You must be worn out.

'It's SuperBoris!'

'Boris has saved us!'

Hop in the back and I'll give you a ride.'

'Off we go!'

There wasn't much room in the trailer, but nobody minded a bit . . .

because they arrived just as
the show was about to start.
The frogs and ducklings loved
the singing, the dancing, and
most of all . . .

they loved Boris for
saving the show!